the Lonely Ones

the Lonely Ones

KELSEY SUTTON

Philomel Books

PHILOMEL BOOKS
an imprint of Penguin Random House LLC
375 Hudson Street
New York, NY 10014

Copyright © 2016 by Kelsey Sutton.

Library of Congress Cataloging-in-Publication Data
Names: Sutton, Kelsey.
Title: The lonely ones / Kelsey Sutton.
Description: New York, NY : Philomel Books, [2016].
Summary: The stress of her father's job loss causes Fain to feel invisible at home and in her new school, but she escapes with the monsters of her imagination until a family crisis and a human friend cause her to reconsider.
Identifiers: LCCN 2015029562 | ISBN 9780399172892 (hardback)
Subjects: | CYAC: Novels in verse. | Loneliness—Fiction. | Family problems—Fiction. | Interpersonal relations—Fiction. | Imagination—Fiction. | BISAC: JUVENILE FICTION / Monsters. | JUVENILE FICTION / Stories in Verse. | JUVENILE FICTION / Social Issues / Physical & Emotional Abuse (see also Social Issues / Sexual Abuse).
Classification: LCC PZ7.5.S88 Lon 2016 | DDC [Fic]—dc23
LC record available at http://lccn.loc.gov/2015029562

Printed in the United States of America.
ISBN 978-0-399-17289-2
10 9 8 7 6 5 4 3 2 1

Edited by Liza Kaplan. Design by Siobhán Gallagher. Text set in 12-point Adobe Jenson Pro.

To Grace Slaubaugh and Randi Georges,
for locking my window.

The Call

Claws scrape
against my windowsill.

Then, a voice,
raspy, childlike, familiar.

It calls my name
and becomes a symphony.

"Fain, are you coming?"
"Come with us, Fain!"
"Wake up!"
"Open your eyes, Fain!"

I try to be firm,
I try to say no.

There's a voice in my head
that whispers I'm getting too old
for these games and adventures.

The ground is so thick with mud
that someone could notice
my tracks.

But my little friends persist
again and again.

Their pleas batter
against my resolve,
until debris crashes down
and I am too weak to resist.

The unbearable truth is
no one will notice my tracks

because no one notices anything.

I take one of their scaly hands;
    a feather tickles against my cheek.

Then I climb outside
and disappear into the night.

Reign

We run through the woods,
more magical
than fireflies or fairies.

     "We love you, Fain," they croon.
                        "You are beautiful."
        "You are a queen."

Their eyes
so adoring,
I can't help but believe them.

They put a scepter in my hand
that glitters with rubies and diamonds.

They place a crown on my head
that feels so light and perfect.

I clutch their talons and hooves and claws,
dance around the fire with wild abandon,
laugh so loud and hard
my lungs burn hotter than the flames.

They are not the frightening ones;
everyone else is.

Reality

The moon fades,
my friends retreat,
the day begins.

Sunlight spills into my room,
     paler and colder
     than yesterday
and I know that
summer is officially over.

I sigh,
leave my bed,
face the fall.

Breakfast is chaotic:
the kitchen becomes
          a street fair
          zoo
          grocery store
everyone clamoring and fighting
for themselves.

The Fredericks are a family
bound only by blood.

Dana smears on lip gloss,
Tyler adjusts his jersey,
Peter shrieks for juice.

Dad holds the paper
in front of his face,
searching the want ads
for someone who will want him back.

Mom pours milk,
so distracted
she does not notice
my dirty feet.

I'm not even trying to hide them.

Beside me
my younger brother frowns,
reaches for the glass
our mother gave him.

It slips off the table—
glass shatters,
liquid runs across the tiles.

Peter blinks,
as if he's surprised and confused
by its fragility.

Someday he'll realize
that anything can break.

An Empty Briefcase, a Dusty Textbook

Not so long ago,
Dad was a car salesman.

He put on a tie and a smile
    went to the dealership
    stood in a parking lot
    talked about Hondas.

A coffee mug rested by his hand
    cold and forgotten
as he showed his customers
where to sign on the dotted line.

Not so long ago,
Mom was a grad student.

She went to class
    sat at a desk
    put pencil to paper
    listened to lectures.

Textbooks rested in her lap
    thick and heavy
as she sat on the couch
learning how to run a business.

Not so long ago,
Dad came through the door
whistling and cheerful,
throwing down his briefcase
to smother us with hugs.

Not so long ago,
Mom devoured words,
smiling and sharing,
putting books aside
to play games or cook.

Then people stopped
buying new cars
and Dad stopped
going to work.

Bills arrived
in the mail
and Mom stared at them
with worried eyes.

No more whistling,
no more hugging,
Dad's briefcase as forgotten
as that cooling cup of coffee.

No more studying,
no more playing,

Mom's smile gone and put away
with those textbooks.

Her notes and classes traded
for a pen and ordering pad.

Dad's office and contracts traded
for the table and job applications.

Now he asks
instead of tells,
sounds desperate
instead of certain.

She smells like grease
instead of books,
looks tired
instead of thoughtful.

Not so long ago,
my mother was a student
and my father was a salesman.

Now
I'm not sure
what they are.

Recession

For weeks and months
I'd heard snatches of conversations,
caught words like
    recession
    hard times
    unpaid
until a short while later
we moved.

The new house
was so old
    so small
    so wilted
like a person marked by wrinkles,
withered by time and memories.

As we
hauled our life inside
in dented boxes,
I stood on the sidewalk
looking up at the place
I was expected to call home.

The windows
watched like eyes,
peering into my sadness and fear.

I tried to imagine
what kind of family
we would become inside those walls,
        so much smaller and fewer
than in the house I'd always known.

"Why do we have to live here?" I'd asked.
"I don't want to move."

My mother sighed,
knelt down in front of me,
touched my cheek.

"Because sometimes," she said,
"people have to do things they don't want to do."

Before I could ask her
what she meant,
Mom stood back up
and went inside.

Leaving me to wonder when
        if ever
people get to do
what they actually want.

Left Behind

For so long
it was just the three of us.

Fain,
Dana,
Tyler.

Skinned knees,
missing teeth,
open roads.

Passing through the sunlit days
in blissful unawareness.

When my legs
couldn't keep up,
they waited
with expectant smiles.

When night fell
and I cowered from the darkness,
they were there
to guide the way.

It happened
so gradually,
I didn't see the changes
until it was too late.

My sister discovered
    mirrors
    phones
    boys.

My brother found
    sports
    parties
    girls.

I tried to follow them
to these new places,
and it shocked me
when I stumbled.

Before long
my siblings had run
so far ahead,
they disappeared from sight.

Innocence

After that
I searched and waited
for someone else
to walk with me.

When she came along,
she wore ribbons
and smelled like sunscreen.

I didn't know
that Katie would be the last friend I'd have
without scales or yellow teeth.

In the summers
Katie's mother would take us to town
and buy us ice cream,
dripping treats that ruined our clothes
                    clung to our skin.

We licked our sticky fingers,
made forever vows.

In those days
forever felt like
such a sweet promise.

Gone

One day
I heard
the rumble of a truck.

When I went to the window
I saw my friend
with the ribbons and forever vows
climbing up, going away.

By the time
I ran outside
it was too late.

She was gone.

I stood there so long,
I felt myself fading
with the sun.

Katie had moved away
and it felt like
the end.

I didn't know that soon
the monsters would arrive
and everything was about
to begin.

Invisible

At first I thought
the people in my life
were too busy
        too distracted
to respond
to the sound of my voice.

Eventually I realized
that they didn't hear me
at all.

It started with my feet,
which slowly disappeared.

Then the rest
began to vanish,
        my legs
        my chest
        my face.

Soon
no one could see me, either.

When I approached others
on the playground,
they looked right through.

When I spoke
to my family,
they didn't raise their gazes.

When my baby brother arrived,
my parents fought,
Dana and Tyler escaped.

All the while
I stood in a corner,
screaming at the top of my lungs.

New Friends

At first being invisible
was terrifying
    sad
      lonely.

Shadows had teeth,
curtains had claws.

I lay in my rickety bed
listening to Dana's snores,
so loud they shook
the world.

Tears dripped onto my sheets
in tiny wet circles,
the only mark of sadness
that anyone could see.

Then one night
a voice hissed, "Don't cry."

Luminous eyes
peered through my window,
but instead of fear,
I only felt wonder.

"What are you?" I asked,
my face drying.

"Friend," the creature replied.
"Come with us."

"Where?"

"To the sky!"

Hesitating,
I told him about the dangers
lurking in the dark.

I didn't know then
that my new friends
were confined to the night.

"But without the dark," the little monster protested,
"you could not see the stars."

So I followed him outside,
enjoyed our time so much
that I ached for those stars
when the morning came
and ate them.

Lunchtime

First day of school,
a new year begins.

Now I turn away
from the sight of my sister
with all her friends,
pretend I don't care
that my classmates find me
strange and awkward.

They don't need to know
that in one brief moment
my hopes
of this year being different
have been dashed against their
uncaring faces.

Outside of our school
that combines every grade and age
I find refuge
beneath a courtyard tree,
focus on the friendly lines
of my notebook.

Getting As is easy;
it's everything else that's hard.

A butterfly lands on my hand,
distracting me from the paper,
and for a wild moment
I'm tempted to rip off its wings.

Humans are capable
of such ugliness.

The creature quivers in the breeze,
unaware that its fate
rests with me.

I stare and stare,
trace the intricate designs on its wings
with my eyes
until the urge passes.

For a few brief moments
I'm at peace.

Then,
without warning,
the butterfly launches itself off my skin
and into the clouds.

Broken Bones

There was a time
when it felt as though
my own wings had been torn off.

I was seven years old,
too young to know about
the uncertainties of growing up.

We were playing a game,
my siblings and I,
trying to capture a flag
made of paper towels and sticks.

The sun was so bright
    the sky so blue
    the birds so euphoric
    our hearts so light.

In a burst of ambition
I leapt toward the flag,
and my brother soared after me,
his arms wrapped around my legs.

We crashed
like a sputtering rocket,
two sounds shattering the air.

A crunch.
A scream.

When we landed
I knew something inside of me
had broken.

I remember the flash of pain,
a burning agony.

There were words filled with alarm
        rushing engines and doors
        white walls and strange smells
        a man with a white coat and cool hands.

At the end of it all
my brother came to me,
laid his head in my lap,
drenched me with tears.

I patted his silken hair
with my good hand,
murmured words of comfort
while our family looked on.

That day I learned
what it is
        to hurt
        to love
        to forgive.

It is a lesson
I have learned
every day since.

The Quarry

I didn't always dread going home.

But when my family
began to collapse
I learned to stay away,
avoid getting trapped
beneath all the debris.

I discovered it on a Tuesday,
a place of comfort
I didn't know I was looking for.

I walked
with my head down,
counting cracks
in the sidewalk
when I noticed the trickle.

It led me
away from the road,
through the trees
to the other side.

The quarry
was gray and kind,
still and quiet;
no deaf ears
or unseeing eyes.

I sat on the hard ground,
pulled out my notebook,
and wrote
of triumph
     wonder
     beauty.

Stories that are
     so vivid
     so real
I could live inside them.

Water lapped against the rocks,
rising and climbing,
trying to escape,
wanting so badly
to be part of something else.

It always fails.

"I know how you feel," I said
to the river that day.

The only reply
was the struggling water,
and that felt
like answer enough.

Shoes and Choices

On the way home from school,
I stop in front of a wide store window,
plumes of breath
swirling from my mouth.

There's an envelope in my hands
containing birthday money
I've been saving
to buy new notebooks.

Passersby
probably think I can't decide
among the shoes on display.

They're right,
but they're wrong, too.

They don't know
that when I helped Peter
put on his shoes this morning,
a toe peeked out at me
through the worn cloth.

I know that Mom and Dad
won't have time to notice,
can't give us what we need.

The money in my hands
could keep my brother warm
or take me to whatever world
I dream up.

Finally I go inside;
a bell over the door
announces my entrance.

"Can I help you?" an employee asks.

His long sideburns
look like wool.

I think of shoes
        of writing
        of choices
        of dreams.

Then
I take a breath
and smile.

"I'm looking for a pair of shoes."

Building

At home,
I show my brother
his new shoes.

He tries them on,
but his interest
is elsewhere.

"Will you build a house with me?"
little Peter asks.

I look down at him,
at the red and yellow building blocks he holds.

Through the closed bedroom door,
I can hear our mother.

She muffles her sobs,
sounds of regret
that we have heard
many times before.

Dana and Tyler have vanished,
become fuzzy and transparent
as they so often do
when I need them most.

I kneel in front of my brother.

"We won't just build a house," I tell him.
"We'll build a whole city."

He smiles.

My mother keeps crying.

Neighbors

Next door
there is another family.

Sometimes
when the sun touches the horizon
I creep through our yards
and watch them through the window.

They eat their perfect dinner
wearing perfect smiles,
filling the stillness
with their perfect words
and unbridled laughter.

Sometimes I stand in full view,
right in front of the glass,
    part of me hoping
    part of me fearing
that they will look up and see me.

They never do.

The Shell

In the room we share,
filled with my sister's posters
and discarded clothes,
there is one thing I despise the most.

The night-light
shaped like a shell.

I wish
I could throw it back
into the ocean.

Dana has always feared the dark
and all that it brings.

There was a time
our mutual wariness
drew us together.

But that was before.

My sister doesn't understand
that without the darkness
we couldn't see the stars.

Night Noises

Every night
as I'm lying in bed
waiting for taps at the window,
the world narrows down
to a smattering of sounds.

A fan whirring
in my parents' room.

My sister snoring
in the next bed.

A clock ticking
in the hallway.

As I listen
I become a part of it all,
    a gust of air
    a hitched breath
    a single moment.

I am suspended,
    hovering above everything
    on top of the world
too big and brave to fall.

So by the time
the magic comes
I've already created
some of my own.

Red Eyes

There is one monster
more gruesome than the rest.

He is a crooked thing
made of rough skin
and red eyes
gleaming with mischief.

Something
that does not belong,
something
just like me.

He was the last one
to press his strange hand against
my bedroom window.

When I asked his name,
the creature only grinned.

He is my favorite.

The Desert

When they tell me
where we're going tonight,
I feel my nose wrinkle
in confusion.

"The desert?" I say. "Why?"

In response,
they whisk me through the neighborhood
    down the streets
    through the city
    past the trees
    toward the edge of the world.

"There's nothing here," I insist.

They tell me
to look closer.

I put my hands on my hips
and look.

This time I see
how endless the horizon is
    how determined the plants are
    how serene the wind feels.

The sand
is cool and hard.

We stand beneath the moon,
watch a tumbleweed
roll by.

In a world
that is constantly moving and shifting,
filled with things that are constantly changing,
this is a place
that doesn't.

My friends are right;
there is beauty
in desolation.

As we stand under the stars,
the distant cry of a coyote
reaches our ears.

We tilt our heads back
and join in its call.

And I swear,
just for a moment,
the moon answers.

Strangers

There was a time
I tried to be silent
as I climbed back into my family's world.

But now
I swing one leg over the sill,
loud and reckless.

I cough,
I stomp,
I sigh.

Dana snores on,
the fan hums,
my parents fight.

Though I do my best not to listen,
sounds drift through
the open door.

She cries accusations,
he mutters insults.

The mattress creaks
when I sit down.

I stare at the wall,
struggling to recognize
the people we've become.

The Dollhouse

Once in a while,
if the arguments are particularly loud
or the silences especially heavy,
I go to the closet
and pull out my dollhouse.

It's old
with beaten corners
and fraying pieces.

The dolls inside
        eyes unblinking
        smiles fixed
remind me of how
things used to be.

A time before want ads
        before my mother cried behind a door
        before my sister spent hours on the phone
        before my brother started kissing and driving.

Once in a while,
I'll reenact scenes
faint in my memory,
of dinners around a table
        movie nights in front of the TV.

The dolls don't avoid one another;
they are magnets
drawn together
again and again.

The house is full
of laughter and light.

Once in a while,
I remember who we used to be.

Once in a while.

Reverence

Besides writing
  and dolls
  and adventures
  and quarries
I find escape
in art class.

In a room
that reeks of paint and ink,
each table contains
only two chairs.

On the first day
I sat in the corner
and waited for someone to claim
the seat next to mine.

The door continually opened,
the room buzzed with chatter,
the teacher told us to be quiet.

That empty seat
filled with my dread;
I tried to distract myself
with a new story.

As I wrote and poured my hopes
into a tale of diamonds and thieves,

the chair creaked;
a boy named Carl
settled beside me.

"Hi," I said.

The word
hovered between us
as Carl hunched over a piece of paper,
wordless and intent,
pen moving furiously.

He draws worlds
the same way I write them:
reverently.

They call him slow
       say he is hollow.

But when I watch Carl,
all I can think
is that an empty person's drawings
would not be so full.

Noticed

A wave of perfume
crashes over me
as Mrs. Olsen
leans close.

"What are you writing?"

No one
has ever bothered
to ask me that question before,
and for a moment
I don't know
how to answer.

I look around,
realize that somehow
I missed the end of English class.

"Just a story," I say
to Mrs. Olsen.

"May I take it home to read?"
she asks.

I don't know
if I want anyone else
to read my words,
gain a peek

into my soul,
but I slowly nod.

She picks the pages up carefully,
holding my heart
in her wrinkled hands.

Beating harder
    louder
    faster.

Then Mrs. Olsen
puts my heart in her desk drawer,
and in that moment
it stops beating entirely.

The Moment

It did not start
on a special day
or at a significant age.

My writing,
my need to create worlds with words,
started with a moment.

Christmas
had come and gone,
and I'd been given a notebook.

For days and months
I carried it everywhere,
bothered by the blank pages
and empty lines.

One afternoon Mom took us to the park,
a place of deep green
and sharp sounds.

She spread out a blanket
        unpacked our lunch.

In the distance
children played tag,

a girl tugged at the strings
of a yellow kite.

Suddenly
Dana and Tyler began to argue,
their voices rising higher
than that toy up in the sky.

Mom shouted,
Peter cried,
insults flew.

The sidewalk to our left
guided a young couple
past our chaotic picnic.

I focused on them,
their ordinary faces
and linked hands.

As if Mom's anger was contagious,
they stopped;
I watched
those two hands
separate.

The girl's face twisted,
the boy's veins jutted.

The boy turned his back
and walked away
without another word or glance.

The girl cried
as she watched him go,
and for a moment
it seemed as if that was it.

But when the boy reached
the end of the sidewalk
he faltered,
and the trees themselves
held their breath.

Slowly,
so slowly,
he turned around and walked back.

She hiccuped and smiled,
they embraced.

My fingers twitched for a pen.

The kite kept flying,
the children kept running,
my family kept fighting.

None of them saw
    knew
    cared.

But it was the first time
I wanted to write
in that notebook,
the first time I realized
there could be more than one ending
to a story.

Gym Class

Balls bounce,
feet pound.

Voices clamor and rise,
as if everyone is fighting for something.

The instructions are to play basketball,
but I can't play
if no one passes to me.

I lose myself
in imaginary worlds until
the ball hits my head
with a deafening *thwack*.

Mary Mosley,
the girl everyone wants to be,
laughs with all her friends.

The sound
echoes in my ears,
and it's all I hear
for the rest of the day.

Lungs

Today
when I arrive at my haven,
lethargic waves
lure me away from my stories.

I lean over
the water that runs through the quarry,
try to submerge myself
in those brown depths,
drown out
all the doubts.

But without my monsters,
I'm not sure
how long I would last
down below.

During the day
my lungs feel
so weak and fragile.

Then it occurs to me that
the ability to breathe
is not the same as
the ability to live.

So I dip my face
below the surface
and stay there
until my fragile lungs
force me to reemerge.

All at once
I am alive.

The Night Shift

My mom
is a woman in mourning.

There are shadows in her voice
as she says good-bye
to my siblings
in the other room.

She's wearing
    the color of grease
    the color of smoke
the black she always wears
as a waitress.

Unaware of my presence,
Mom enters the kitchen.

She puts one hand on the doorknob;
Dad stands to kiss her cheek.

She pretends not to see him
and shuts the door behind her.

Freak

All night I watch Dana
talk on the phone,
curling her finger through the wire.

When she catches me watching
my sister turns away.

"Nothing," she says. "Fain is just being a freak."

Then she stretches her legs
toward the ceiling,
aiming for sky.

My sister doesn't know
that I've already been there.

Encounters

Leaving Dana
to her endless conversation,
I take my post by the window
to wait for moonlight
     silence
     friends.

A red scarf
flies and swirls
down the street,
followed moments later
by a frantic girl.

Without thinking,
I jump up
     run down the stairs
     throw open the door
     dive down the sidewalk
into the twilight.

The scarf tucks itself
around my ankles,
as if it was looking for me all along.

Breathless,
the girl stops short.

Her hair
is the same color
as the scrap of material
in my hands.

"Oh, thank you,"
she says.

Suddenly I recognize her:
my neighbor,
the girl who sits at the table
with her family every night.

The one I watch
        envy
                wonder about.

With a smile,
I hold out the scarf.

She quickly takes it and turns away,
but it's too late;
I glimpse the sadness in her eyes.

"Thanks again," she blurts,
runs back to her house
before I can answer.

The door slams
but I'm frozen in place,
thinking about that once-perfect family.

Maybe
I'm not the only one
with monsters outside my window.

The Jungle

That night
I wait.

When the numbers
on the clock read 12:00,
my little friends arrive.

As always,
they announce their presence
with sounds and taps.

I drop eagerly
from the sill
and the curtains flutter
like fingers reaching for me
even after I'm gone.

I gasp when I see it:
the forest behind my house
has become a jungle.

Plunging inside
without hesitation,
we run and weave
through leaves and vines,
more wild than anything around us.

I hear the roar of a tiger,
the calls of a toucan,
the screeches of a dozen monkeys.

We climb a great tree,
swing alongside them,
imitate their calls.

It would be so easy
to get lost
in this place
of green chaos.

When the sun
touches the horizon
I follow my friends home,
grateful that someone
can show me the way.

Kissing

On my way to class
I spot a familiar figure,
someone with my golden hair
and a thirst for something more
than we've been given.

My brother has a girl
pressed up against his locker.

It's Iris Anderson,
a cheerleader with flawless skin
that other girls probably imagine
ripping off and putting on as their own.

She giggles,
and for a moment
I forget that it's strange
to be watching my brother like this.

I have never understood kissing,
the lure of lips and slobber,
the meaning of tongues and heat.

It looks as though
he is searching for something
in her mouth.

I wonder
if he'll like what he finds.

Mary Mosley

While everyone
        eats their sandwiches
        drinks their milk
        chatters loudly
I sit silently beneath my tree.

Carl rests in the grass
far from everyone else,
drawing as always.

The blank pages in my lap
        quiver
as if to get my attention.

I am too busy
staring at Mary Mosley
and her friends
to write anything.

Like every other day,
they talk and laugh.

I imagine myself
talking and laughing, too.

But I never noticed until now
my neighbor
sitting with them.

She sees me staring,
quickly looks away.

"That girl is by herself,"
        I hear her say
        about me.
"I feel bad for her."

"She's too quiet," Mary replies.
"It's like she's plotting our demise."

The others laugh,
all except my neighbor,
who is entirely focused
on plucking a blade of grass
free from the ground.

I want to inform them
that I am not silent
because I have nothing to say.

I am silent
because no one is listening.

Change

After lunch,
someone new joins the class.

He stands up front,
fidgeting nervously,
and tells us about
life in New Orleans.

The boy is beautiful.

His voice is a soft drawl
that I could wrap around myself
like a blanket.

His face
is a story
waiting to be told.

Afterward,
as I gather my books,
he turns in my direction.

"Hi, I'm Matthew," he says.

I glance over my shoulder.

Heart pounds—
I realize

no one else is there,
he is looking at me.

Suddenly
          I miss being invisible
yet suddenly
          I never want
          to be unseen again.

When I say nothing,
he asks for my name.

"Fain," I whisper.

"Fain," he repeats.

But I hardly hear him;
I am a balloon
filling with air and light,
floating up
                    and up
                                        and up.

When I look down,
Matthew seems so small.

I hover in the air,
realize I want to hear the words
coming out of his mouth.

My feet touch the ground,
and it feels more solid
than ever before.

The River

I am rushing,
whooshing over and under
    this way and that
eager to escape the school walls
and get to the quarry.

I burst through the doors,
stop short at the sight
of Carl sitting on the lawn.

He looks so content,
even as everyone walks around him
like a current slipping past a stone.

He bends over his sketchbook,
drawing with such fervor
that the river of rumbling buses
and shouting students
doesn't hinder the strokes
of his pen.

I begin to take a step toward him—
a car honks.

Carl closes his sketchbook,
stands,
hurries off.

I stand there,
alone on the shore,
and watch the waters run.

Echoes

It is one thing
to be alone
because there's no alternative.

It is something else entirely
to choose this isolation.

I stand in the quarry,
gazing out at the water.

"How are you?" I shout
into the vastness.

"How are you?" it screams back.

I don't know what to say,
not quite sure how I feel,
so I don't respond to the quarry's call.

In this place,
it's much easier
to believe that someday
I might have an answer.

I sit down
    open my notebook
    and write.

Stories

The scribbles of my pen
bring close everything
that is out of reach.

I write
    about a girl
    who is great at basketball.

I write
    about a girl
    who sits with others during lunch.

I write
    about a girl
    with a loud voice and a smile that beams.

I write
    about a girl
    who has no time or need
    for solitude and quarries.

I write
    about a girl
    who demands to be seen.

These stories
might be realistic for some.

For me,
they're only fantasy.

Drowning

She lies still;
the setting sun casts
a dark silhouette
onto the couch and floor.

"Mom?" I ask.

Silence
is her reply.

She's become a statue,
permanently frosted
like the winter glass.

Then a voice so faint,
as though it's folding
back inside of her
like a flower hiding from the cold:
"It's just so hard sometimes."

"What is?" I ask.

Another second of quiet,
full of so much unsaid
that it feels as though
we're drowning.

Then Mom
utters a strange laugh,
disappears into her room.

She doesn't come back
with a rope or a life jacket.

I sink slowly into the depths.

Sunken Ships

That night I soar
through the ocean deep,
a world as powerful and blue
as a tear.

My hair
billows around my head
like golden seaweed.

Bubbles flow from my monsters' mouths
as they shriek and laugh and play.

"Treasure, treasure!" I know they are saying.

We are whale riders
     explorers
     hunters
until suddenly
we are not alone.

Mermaids croon in my ear,
voices soft as their scales are hard.

Together
we are a parade
of danger and beauty.

We swim to where
a ship waits for us,
buried in sand and time.

We explore every part of it,
grinning with excitement
when we find piles of gold coins
                        sparkling jewels.

Without greed or intent,
the mermaids and monsters and me
sift through the treasure,
watch it float around us,
rich and triumphant in every way.

Time seems to slow,
and I know
I'm running out of air.

The sun is coming;
I must return to the surface
where I belong.

Praise

After class on Monday,
Mrs. Olsen pulls me aside.

My story
rests quietly
in her hand.

She tells me about a contest
I should enter,
a magazine that publishes
the best short stories,
that I need a teacher to sponsor me,
she'd be happy to do it.

A lump grows
in my throat,
until I can hardly
ask the question
burning on the tip of my tongue.

"Is it really good enough?" I say
around the flames.

Mrs. Olsen
puts her fingers on my shoulder
and squeezes.

"No," she answers.

"It's *better.*"

Matthew

"Hi, Fain."

The sound of that voice
jerks my head upward.

The pain
is worth it.

Matthew stands next to my tree,
smiling down at me,
shifting from foot to foot,
hair falling into his eyes.

"How are you?" he asks.

It feels like
I was born without a tongue.

I clutch my notebook tighter,
wish I was clever or dazzling
like Mary Mosley and her friends,
and mumble the answer he expects,
something shapeless and simple.

Matthew sits on the grass
without invitation,
startling me so badly
I almost run.

Matthew leans back,
closes his eyes.

I pretend to write,
steal glances at him through my lashes.

My heart races fast and loud;
I wonder if he hears it.

"What are you doing?"

Even though he's now the second person
to ask me this question,
I still feel the shock of it
        his curiosity
        his sincerity
in my bones.

"Writing," I whisper.

He grins,
tells me that's cool,
and for the rest of lunch
we sit together,
talk about my stories.

Matthew confesses
his difficulty with writing and English.

"I can help with that," I say
eagerly.

He grins again,
we both grow quiet.

He enjoys
the breeze,
I enjoy
the view.

But I keep wondering
why he would want to sit beside
someone like me?

Matthew turns his head,
catches me staring,
reads the confusion
on my face,
hears the unspoken question.

"They're just so loud," he says,
glancing toward our peers
doing cartwheels on the lawn,
hiding their insecurities
behind cheer
        laughter
        superiority.

I smile,
almost tell him that if silence
is what he likes,
I'll never say another word.

A Moment

The sky fills with gray
and I know
walking home
or to the quarry
would be foolish.

I call my mother;
she surprises me by answering.

I wait by the curb
until she pulls up
in a burst of smoke and sound.

Time alone with my mother
has always been rare.

Now, finally,
I have her attention.

I could ask her anything,
about the future or the past.

But all I want to mention
is the contest.

"Mom?" I say.

She takes a second too long
to respond.

A moment
is all it takes
to lose courage.

Without taking her eyes
off the road,
she says, "Yes?"

Even the growing darkness
can't hide the weariness
in her voice.

I give in,
hear myself ask her
what's for dinner.

"Macaroni," she says.

I force an excited smile,
as if we haven't had it
twice already this week.

Then I turn my head away,
watch rain quiver
down the glass.

Perishable

My brother asks for a snack,
so I walk to the fridge
    open the door
    bathe in its light.

Scant shelves
peer back at me,
begging to give them
purpose again.

I open a drawer,
find some forgotten fruit
    green oranges
    brown apples.

I feel a kinship
with these perishable things,
these foods that have waited,
been neglected for so long.

And I wonder
if my family knows
that when we're not careful
    not quick enough
things will fall to rot and ruin
        so far
        so badly
they can't be saved.

I cut out the bad parts,
hand what's left of the apple
to little Peter.

He beams at me
as if it's the sweetest thing
he's ever tasted.

Another Storm

From our place
on the faded carpet,
Peter and I balance blocks.

The stillness is disrupted
by a rumbling of thunder
        a trembling of everything.

I look to the window
but the sky is clear,
a serene shade of orange
that fades into pink.

My father bursts into the room
like a clap of lightning,
whooping and waving the phone around.

"I have an interview!" he shouts.

Without warning
he drops the phone
        picks up Peter
        grabs my hand
and begins to dance.

Mom stands in the doorway,
grumbles, "About time."

Peter's tower
tumbles down.

Dad's hips swing
from side to side;
Mom looks on
without smile or cheer.

Hers is the face of lightning,
threatening to strike,
destroy our hope.

My lips twitch
with uncertainty
and Dad's eyes are so bright,
they are painful to look at.

But this storm of happiness
soon sweeps over me and Peter
until all three of us
are drenched.

We spin in dizzying circles,
and I secretly pray
we won't need an umbrella.

Fairy Tales

Tonight my friends
greet me with a request.

"Tell us a story," they beg.

In my backyard
      transformed to sandy beach
we sit in a circle
by the glinting sea,
listen to air whistling through the rocks.

"Once upon a time," I begin,
because that's how the best stories
always begin,
"there was a girl."

       "You!"
    "It's you!"
       "The girl is you!"

"Shhh," I say, grinning,
and tell them a story
of hope and trees and New Orleans.

As my mouth moves I gaze up at the moon,
thinking of how similar we are.

One side always hidden
while the other
shines so bright.

Yearning

Every day this week
the boy from New Orleans sits with me.

His eyes are sunlight,
my stomach is a garden in bloom.

Sometimes our words
float light as air;
sometimes our quiet
sits heavy as stone.

There are days
we work on
his English homework,
sitting so close
our elbows nearly
touch.

Afterward
I am so full
of thoughts about Matthew,
the pages of my notebook
remain empty
in my lap.

Impatience

After class the next day
I ask Mrs. Olsen
if she's heard anything from the magazine
about my story.

"Patience," she says
with a wink.

Frustration bubbles up
inside me.

I want to tell her
that I'm tired of waiting,
that all I do is wait
      for my peers to notice
      for my family to hear
      for the moon to rise.

It feels as though
I'll be withered and gray
by the time this wait is over.

But I smile at Mrs. Olsen
like nothing is wrong
and walk away.

Rocks

My parents' tension
has turned to shouts
that echo through the night.

I stand on our lawn
throwing rocks at the stars,
hoping my aim is good
so that I can make a wish.

A wish that things
would change.

But if there's one thing I've learned
in this terrifying world
    where everything is big
      and I am so small
it's that stars don't fall on their own.

We must knock them

d
o
w
n.

Desire

It seems
my wish has come true . . .
in part.

Something *has* changed.

But I should have been more careful
with the hopes I pinned
on that falling star,
because that something
is not anything I like.

In math class today,
Matthew laughs
at one of Mary Mosley's jokes.

She is not funny,
she is not a queen
with a gleaming crown
or a glittering scepter.

But still Matthew laughs.

I am so distracted
by the happy crinkles around his eyes
that I forget the story
I was excited to write
only a few seconds ago.

Then our teacher
passes out a test
and I realize—
I've been so distracted by
        fighting parents
        writing stories
        helping Matthew
        making wishes
—I forgot to study.

I sit still
        worried
        helpless
as stone,
grip the edge of the desk so hard,
my knuckles turn white.

The test lands in front of me,
but my eyes stay on
Matthew and Mary.

We are victims
of our own desires.

Risks

Test over,
my answers only guesses,
I hurry out of class.

In the hallway
I see a shock of red hair
    like the scarf in the middle of the road
and stop.

She stands next to the lockers
surrounded by friends,
but somehow
my neighbor still looks alone.

Our eyes meet
and she lifts her hand
in a tentative wave.

None of the others
seem to notice.

I hesitate,
    a pause longer
        than days or months or years.
Wonder what would happen
if I waved back, said hello.

Will she one day
        move away
        find someone
        or something
better?

I think about
falling stars and wishes
while my neighbor waits
with hopeful eyes.

Then I take a breath
        close my eyes
        make a choice
        take a risk
and wave back.

Metal Birds

After school,
the silence of the quarry
is shattered
by the rumblings of a plane.

I look up from my pages,
track the movement
with my eyes.

It leaves
a white stain
across the sky;
I wonder who is sitting
in those seats.

I think about those people
    where they're going
    what they want.

For a few moments,
I picture myself
within that metal bird
    flying away
    soaring high.

But then
I come back down.

I always come back
                    d
                       o
                          w
                             n.

The Peak

Later,
a scratching sound
interrupts my dreams.

I open my eyes
and smile into the red ones
of my favorite monster.

"Where are we going?" I ask him.

The rest crowd behind
with mischievous smirks
        glowing eyes
            twitching talons and wings and claws.

My sister snores,
unaware of them poking and licking
her sleeping skin.

I ask them
if we are going
into the woods again.

                "Better!"
        "Up!"
                    "Climb, climb, climb!"

Bed abandoned
    blankets tossed aside
    warmth forgotten
I follow them
    out the window
    through the trees
    toward the mountain
that once was the hill
in my backyard.

Wind nibbles and whispers;
I crane my neck,
try to see the top of the rock
even as the night sky
keeps it hidden.

I hesitate;
snow swirls all around.

My friends are already climbing,
calling down to me.

I summon courage,
begin the ascent,
haul and strain
up the side of the mountain.

They shout encouragement on either side,
howl like a pack of wolves.

The higher I get,
the sharper
the cold's teeth.

Finally,
gasping and burning,
I stand tall on the peak.

My head brushes
against the moon.

The monsters shriek and dance,
their voices echo in delight.

I don't move
for a few moments,
enjoy the stillness,
listen to the stars
murmur my name.

Then I spread my arms,
close my eyes,
and fly.

The Lonely Ones

Once
I asked them why.

Out of all the children
in all the world,
why they chose to
tap

      scrape

             claw
on *my* window.

"Because you're lonely," they answered.
"We look for the lonely ones."

The Puppet

Sunlight shines down
on my blank pages.

In the brief space of time
before Matthew arrives,
I wait beneath my tree.

My neighbor walks past.

Today she stops
    clears her throat
    looks at me.

"Hi," she says. "I'm Anna."

Before I can give her
a piece of myself
in return,
someone calls her name
and she hurries away.

It's as if she is a puppet
and someone has jerked her strings.

Anna sits with Mary Mosley,
wears a smile so big
it looks painful.

My mouth has forgotten how
to do such a thing
until Matthew appears
and it remembers.

Home

My father sits at the kitchen table,
head in his hands,
  jobless
    sleepless
      hopeless.

He doesn't have to tell us
that he didn't get the job.

With bleary eyes
he goes to the fridge,
pulls out a beer.

Mom comes in;
the fighting starts.

I go upstairs
  sit by my bedroom window
and wait for the sky to darken.

One Giant Leap for Fain

Tonight my friends tell me
we are going to the moon.

"How do we get there?" I ask.

    "Jump!"
        "As high as you can."
            "Leap into the air!"

We link hands
like cutout paper figures
    bend our knees
    count to three.

I keep my eyes open
the entire time
to watch the world
shoot past—
    or am I
    shooting past the world?

We land,
    feet bouncing off the ground
    stars glittering
    everything glowing.

The Earth seems so far away
    so gently blue

that I struggle to remember
why living there is so hard.

Then,
for hours or days,
we float through the weightless air.

I only remember
who I am and where we are
when my favorite monster
tugs at my nightgown.

"You dropped this," he hisses,
holding one sock in his claws.

I smile
and close his fist
around it.

"Who needs socks," I say,
"when your feet don't touch the ground?"

Seasons

In the morning,
I hit the ground
with a jarring *thud*.

The F at the top of my test
is so red,
it looks like the paper is bleeding.

I know
that thoughts of Matthew
  sleepless nights
are to blame.

Our teacher keeps talking
and everyone else keeps listening;
some of them
hold shiny grades.

I slump,
prop my chin on my hand,
turn my head.

Through the window
I see flowers begin to shrivel
and the world turn to brown.

An Offer

There are so few things
that make sense
and countless things
that don't.

I sit beneath my tree,
stare so hard at that F,
the paper should have holes.

The apple in my hand feels rotten
    goes uneaten.

"Tell your parents," the teacher said.
"We need a signature."

The fear in my eyes
must have been obvious,
like a bleeding wound
or a broken heart.

She might think this will
disappoint my parents,
but the truth is
I'm worried it won't.

Suddenly
movement above me,
a familiar scent

of shampoo
of kindness
of possibility
taunts my senses.

"Hi," Matthew says.

"Hi," I say in return.

I resist the urge
to pat my hair,
fix my shirt,
and hope I look pretty
in this slant
of sunlight.

The red-marked test
catches the wind
and Matthew's eye.

"Math? I can help you with that."

For a few seconds
my heart stops beating;
I don't tell Matthew
I'm good at math,
that failing tests
isn't something
I normally do.

Instead,
another person with my voice
whispers, "Okay."

He grins
        takes a bite
        of my apple.

I can feel Mary Mosley's glare.

The most beautiful girl
        jealous
that the most beautiful boy
is sitting with me.

Matthew hands back the apple,
and when he's not looking,
I bite out of the same spot he did.

For the first time,
I understand
the purpose of a kiss.

Good Listener

I arrive at Matthew's
with a heart full of hope.

It feels
strange and wonderful
to go somewhere new—
    not the sky
    up a mountain
    through the desert
but here on Earth.

I won't be missed at home.

The place where he lives
is as perfect as he is with
    paved streets
    prim trees
    elegant mailboxes.

A green door
beckons.

I raise a trembling fist,
knock three times,
feel vibrations
in every bone.

Before I can prepare
or even take a breath
Matthew is there,
smiling at me with those sky-blue eyes.

"Come in," he says.

I step over the threshold,
inhale his intoxicating smell
as it rolls off his skin.

We walk through the empty house;
he leads me to his room.

I wonder for the thousandth time
if he can hear my pulse,
wild and erratic.

A goldfish
swims round and round
on Matthew's desk.

"That's Good Listener," he tells me
with a sheepish grin.

"What do you tell him?" I ask,
settling down beside Matthew,
so tense that my spine
has become a plank of wood.

The boy from New Orleans
    frowns
    wrinkles his brow
    then says, "I tell him the things no one else wants to hear."

All I can think
    as Matthew opens a textbook
    teaches me about numbers
is that I am jealous
of a goldfish.

Do Better Next Time

No more delaying,
no more avoiding.

I walk home from Matthew's house,
find my father
in the kitchen.

Without an excuse or explanation,
I lay the bleeding test
on the table in front of him.

He barely glances my way,
just mutters, "Do better next time."

My response
is so faint,
it's barely a breath
of air.

"I will."

We sit in silence,
the air as cold in here
as it is
out there.

The tree
beyond the kitchen window
rustles in the wind.

Leaves curl and wither
till the branches are almost bare.

Trees
always know when to let go
and when to start again.

If only people
were so smart.

Daydreams

There are days
I imagine
everything opposite.

People walk on ceilings
    pour upward
    cry inward.

My mother asks to read my stories,
my father tells me that he's proud.

There is nothing outside my window
but leaves and stars and air.

I have
never felt lonely.

Out to Sea

That night
I open my window
to a world of
lapping waves
and endless depths.

My friends
drift by on a boat,
waving urgently,
calling for me
to jump.

I land on deck
with a squeal.

The moon and stars
loom close enough
to touch.

All around me
everything familiar
has vanished.

No roads
    or houses
    or trees.

We run
to the bow
    grab hold of ropes
    lean over so far
we could easily fall.

"Look down, look down!" the monsters shriek.

I gaze
into the darkness below,
see the hulking shape
of something that lives
in the water.

The shape moans—
a whale!
—its mournful greeting
touches my soul.

Suddenly
the sky flashes.

I jerk back,
my friends
begin to clamber
for the ropes.

"A storm!"
                "A storm is coming!"
                                "Hurry, hurry!"

We work together,
turn the boat around,
leave the whale behind.

Once we reach the house,
I climb violently inside.

Dana snores away
in the corner.

The monsters shout their good-byes,
sail away
between one lightning bolt
and the next.

I slam the window down;
rain pounds against the glass.

In the Hallway

I don't see her;
our shoulders crash together
in a painful meeting
of skin and bone.

Mary Mosley
whirls to face me.

"You're the girl helping Matthew," she says
with narrowed eyes.

I rub my shoulder,
say, "I'm Fain."

"Fain," she repeats. "What kind of name is that?"

I don't know what to say
    how to respond
but it doesn't matter.

She's already
turned around
    moved on
        forgotten.

Constellations

I hear the sounds
as I approach.

I'm returning from a trip
to the wilds of Africa
and discover the war in my house raging on.

I stay outside
where it is easier to pretend
things are different
      better.

Tyler and Dana
are off doing the same,
having adventures of their own
without me.

I'm standing on the lawn,
stones heavy in my hand,
when she approaches.

"What are you doing?" Anna asks.

Before I can answer,
the voices of my parents
      hard and desperate as a knife
slice through the air.

For a moment
we just watch them.

They stand in front of
the wide window,
exposing our war to the world.

Anna steps closer,
her expression unreadable
in the moonlight.

She says, "That's the Little Dipper,"
finger pointed to the sky.

I follow with my eyes,
but I don't find utensils or simplicity
in the smattering of stars.

I see something else entirely.

That maybe,
just maybe,
I'm not so alone after all.

"Do you see it?" my neighbor questions.

She looks at the sky,
I look at her.

"I see it," I lie.

Visitor

Today
my time at the quarry,
my solace and writing,
is interrupted
by a fox.

It picks its way
over the rocks,
sniffing at the water
and the air.

I stare at it for
a while,
but it doesn't
notice me.

I go still,
hardly dare
to breathe.

I watch it
for a few minutes,
admire its grace
and strength.

We have so much in common,
this creature and I.

Both alone
    cautious
    quiet.

We learn
    think
    explore.

Just beneath the surface
we are each a stealthy breed,
staying out of sight of others
whenever we feel threatened.

But whenever people look at us,
they only see
Fain or fox.

Congratulations

Three words
I will never forget.

Three words
I will frame in my head like a picture.

"You won, Fain,"
my teacher says.

She puts the letter down
on the table,
the letter that says

Congratulations.

Mrs. Olsen
    tells the class I won
    makes the class clap
    says my story will appear in a magazine.

I sit there,
stunned,
basking in the sun of this moment.

For the first time
since the monsters appeared,
I don't want night to come.

Ecstasy

Nothing
can touch me.

I float
through the hallways,
oblivious
to Mary Mosley and her friends.

I stand
in gym class,
unfazed
by whacking balls and deep sneers.

I drift
to the courtyard,
unaware
of my sister's presence.

All that matters
is my story.

I am no longer invisible.

Mother, Look

I ride the bus home,
        Congratulations
in my hands.

Walk through the front door
to find a familiar scene:
Mom resting on the couch,
one hand tucked against her cheek.

Peter sits on the rug,
distracting himself
with blocks.

They don't know
my wish has come true—
that everything has changed.

"Are you awake?" I whisper.
"Can I show you something?"

The magazine liked it,
I want to tell her.
*Someone found it worthy
of first place.*

Before she can answer,
Peter's pile of blocks
topples over.

I feel the collapse
inside my soul.

Mom's eyes snap open,
irritation written
between red veins.

"Careful, careful," she says,
as if saying something twice
will make it heard
        make it matter.

"Look, look,"
I say.

She closes her eyes.

Light

Tonight we explore
caves buried deep beneath
the earth.

The ceilings are low,
something drips
in the distance.

I follow my friends,
heart pounding
louder than any echo.

It's as though
every light in the world
has gone out
and nothing beautiful
could possibly exist
down here.

Finally
we reach complete darkness,
too thick and cold
to bear.

I hesitate,
draw back,
tell them
I don't want to go any farther.

"Just to those big rocks," they insist,
clicking and scrabbling
along the stone floor.

Nervous,
scared to be alone,
I follow them
reluctantly.

Just when I think
I can't go another step,
I see it.

Up ahead,
a single light,
blinking like a beacon.

One light
turns into dozens
        hundreds
        thousands.

Green and glowing,
like tiny galaxies
hidden far underground.

We take hold
of one another
and walk through space.

130

Later,
after I've climbed into bed,
I think about how
beauty can be found
in the most unexpected
of places.

Notes

A piece of paper
lands on my desk,
made of sharp edges
and possibility.

Matthew smiles at me
as my fingers
unfold his words.

His handwriting
is boyish and small
and I want to tattoo it
on my skin.

Have you ever seen such a horrible toupee?

A giggle escapes me,
so unexpected
there's no way to stop it.

Mr. Pars
spins toward me,
his scowl as crooked
as the piece of hair
adorning his scalp.

"Is there something funny about particles?" he demands.

I bite the insides of my cheeks
to keep from smiling,
shake my head.

He turns away
and Matthew makes a face
behind his back.

I laugh so hard,
I don't even care
when Mr. Pars
yells at me again.

Anna

After dinner
I lie in the dry grass,
face tilted toward
the sky.

I hear a door open,
feel someone rustle
the grass beside me.

At first
neither of us speaks.

Then,
as if she's been holding on
to the words
        too tight
        too long
Anna tells me
how her parents
try so hard
to make everything perfect.

I tell her
how my parents don't try
to do anything at all.

One house full of false cheer,
the other swollen with silence.

It feels easier speaking
to someone I hardly know
with only the twilight sky
as my witness.

After all,
nothing bad can happen
once the sun has gone down.

A Candle

After the quarry
when I come home
from school the next day
our house is dark,
everything shrouded
in shadow.

But there is nothing hidden
about the fight
between my parents.

White lips,
red eyes,
blue veins,
their anger I can see
as they argue
about who was supposed to pay the electric bill.

A horn honks outside,
Dana rushes out.

Music crackles through the air,
Tyler's door slams.

I huddle in my room with Peter,
whisper
of mermaids and mountains and dragons.

But I don't tell him
how much I enjoy the darkness,
how the night
is where I truly belong.

How it makes some things easier to hide
        others more difficult to find
how it gives the feared and misunderstood
        a place of comfort and understanding.

Then Mom comes in
with a candle.

Pale and silent,
she leaves us
with its light.

I resist the temptation
to blow it out.

Phone Calls

Days pass,
leaves darken.

I sit with Matthew,
forget the quarry.

I talk with Anna,
don't hold back.

Then
the phone rings.

"Here."

My sister
relinquishes it,
impatience written
in the lines of her face.

I stare at her,
some part of my mind
certain this is a trick or a lie.

Dana says my name,
shakes the phone in my face
till I take it.

"I'm bored," Matthew announces in my ear.
"Talk to me."

I press his voice
to my head so hard
it hurts.

> He dialed my number.
> He called me.
> He wants to talk to me.

"What should I say?" I breathe,
slipping away
so no one else can hear,
not monsters
or parents
or siblings.

The boy from New Orleans laughs and says,
"Tell me anything."

I smile
and tell him everything.

Nursery Rhymes

They're leaning against the lockers
when I walk past.

It starts quietly,
snippets sung under the breath
until it swells from a trickle of water
to a dull roar.

Mary's voice,
the loudest.

"Fain, Fain, go away," they chant.

I hunch my shoulders
and hurry to class.

But not before
I see Anna
standing among them.

Knights of Old

As the rest of my family
slumbers and dreams,
I am wild and awake.

A castle awaits
in the backyard,
towering over my house
like a giant.

When the clock sounds
I join my friends,
who whisper
of a dangerous beast.

We rush through the night
with armor that
    clanks like a drum
    shines like a star
    protects like a stone.

Past the gates
the dragon crouches,
rumbling the ground
with the strength
of its growl.

I clutch the hilt of my sword
and we storm the hall

like knights of old,
shining and bright and true.

Flames climb the walls,
    blackening
    burning
    reaching.

We duck our heads
and press on,
wielding our weapons
with discordant cries.

The chamber is high and wide,
swallowing the sounds of battle,
    the clang of metal
    the bellow of the beast.

There is no mercy here,
there is no hesitation.

But as soon as I pierce the dragon,
see it lying there with heaving sides
                resigned eyes
I feel a twinge of regret.

Outsiders

Somehow
the end of October has arrived
without any of us noticing,
like loneliness or sorrow.

On the night
of candy and costumes
our parents are busy,
too busy to take Peter out.

Dana and Tyler
are busy, too,
busy avoiding the house.

My heart aches
to see my baby brother
press his face to the window,
watching families
        witches
        superheroes
        princesses
pass by.

He shouldn't be
        stuck inside looking out
        on the outside looking in.

The other children laugh loudly,
    buckets clanking
    wrappers crinkling
    doorbells ringing.

For a few minutes
I watch Halloween go on without us.

Then I run,
find a pair of scissors,
yank the sheets up
off my bed.

There are some things
we have the power to change.

Trick or Treat

We step outside just as
Anna walks past.

Marker lines
sweep across her cheeks
like whiskers.

"Hey," she says,
"mind if I tag along?"

I almost agree,
but then I hear Mary's cruel words
in my head,
see Anna standing beside her
doing nothing.

"Maybe next year," I tell her.

Hurt flashes across Anna's face
like a bolt of lightning,
there and gone so quickly
I wonder if I imagined it.

Then door to door we go,
me and Peter the ghost,
        clutching sticky hands
        seeking treats and childhood.

Though his costume
hides his face,
I can feel his smile
pulse through.

I'm so focused on Peter,
it takes me a while to notice
something moving in the shadows,
        the swish of a tail
        the sound of a growl
such sure signs
that my friends are following me.

But I don't crave
their presence tonight.

We turn the corner,
bump into Dana
having fun with her friends.

"What are you supposed to be?"
my sister demands,
eyeing my jeans and sneakers.

"Myself," I answer.

Disapproval
tugs at her mouth,
and I realize
she has no idea who that is.

Invitation

On Wednesday a voice says,
"Mary is throwing a party. Want to go?"

These words are foreign to me,
        always wrapped and gifted
            to someone else.

I'm so startled by their weight
that at first
I don't react.

Someone kicks
the bottom of my shoe.

"Earth to Fain."

I come down
        come to
            look up
at Matthew's handsome face.

"A party?"

He squats down,
leans forward,
touches my cheek.

I freeze.

"You had an eyelash," he explains,
holding it out,
urging me to make a wish.

I shake my head,
let the wind take it.

"I don't need to anymore."

Love Is

the final words
of a story.

my little brother's
dimpled smile.

warm socks
after a trek through the snow.

one more fry
in the bottom of the bag.

the *tap-tap-tap*
of a monster at the window.

being noticed
after feeling invisible for so long.

the way Matthew
looks at me.

Restless

Something feels different
about the quarry
today.

But when I look around,
nothing appears
changed.

The water is still,
the rocks are gray,
the sky is pale.

It isn't until
I'm on my way home
that I realize:
the quarry
doesn't feel like an escape
anymore.

It feels
like a hiding place.

Sick

There's no fighting
in the house tonight.

My mother's hands
cup Peter's face
as though he is made of glass.

"He's too hot," she keeps saying
over and over.

They take his temperature
and the house shrinks.

Tears streak down
Peter's face,
his mouth wide open,
the sound of sirens coming out.

"Stay here," Dad orders,
keys in one hand,
Peter in the other.

My mother trails behind them;
she has never looked so small.

None of us speak
as the door slams.

All that's left
is fear
    silence
        and a red-hot thermometer.

Waiting

Back and forth,
wall to wall,
left to right.

I watch Dana worry,
I watch Tyler pace,
I watch the clock tick.

When the phone rings,
its sharp sound makes us jump.

Dana answers breathlessly.

"How is he?"
"How long?"
"Where?"

The hum of my father's voice responds,
and at the end of the conversation
my sister faces us.

Her brown eyes
have turned to black.

"They're not coming home tonight."

Worry

So much can change
in a matter of
    seconds
    hours
    days.

I sit on my bed,
hold Peter's costume tight,
think about how cold it was
when I took him trick-or-treating.

Dana flies into the room,
a burst of color and sound.

She draws up short
at the sight of me
clutching a sheet with holes.

Something changes
in her eyes.

"He's going to be okay," she tells me.

"Promise?" I ask.

But I know my sister can't
guarantee such things.

Dana settles down beside me,
touches the sheet
as if Peter
is still beneath it.

A pause.

Then,
"Promise."

Hugh the Weatherman

The next day
I rush home, hoping to find
Mom on the couch with the remote,
Peter on the floor with his blocks.

When I enter the living room,
see that it's empty,
I fight hard not to cry.

My older siblings
arrive home minutes later;
we sink onto the couch,
wait for the phone to ring.

Suddenly
Tyler jumps up,
moves toward the door.

"You can't leave!" Dana snaps.

He hesitates,
glances from us
to his escape.

Reluctantly
he returns,
drums fingers against his thighs
in a restless beat.

The three of us
sit silently
on the threadbare couch
until Dana reaches for the remote.

We stare at the TV
as though it holds
the answers to our questions.

Hugh the weatherman
tells us about the gloomy tomorrows
we should expect.

My siblings' hands rest
on either side of me;
I reach for them
as if grasping
for a lifeline.

Another silence follows
that even Hugh can't seem to fill.

But neither of my siblings
pulls away.

Snow

Two days pass,
torturous and slow.

Dad stops home,
picks up clothes
for him and Mom,
gives us money for pizza,
heads back to the hospital.

On the second night
without Peter
Tyler says my name,
points to the window.

The sky is coming apart,
drifting to the ground
in fluffy white pieces.

Suddenly
Dana jumps up,
turns on the radio,
grabs my hands
and our protesting brother's.

We go round
and round
until colors blend and feelings blur.

The snowflakes
float with us,
silent and steady,
performing a dance of their own.

I want to ask my siblings
why we can't do this
all the time.

Instead I keep dancing
        keep laughing
as the snow keeps falling.

Not Tonight

A hiss,
a growl,
a squawk.

The monsters at my window
press against the glass,
desperate to get my attention.

    "Fain, let's go to Mars!"
                  "Explore the jungle."
        "Raft down the river!"

I turn on my side,
my back to them,
    feel my siblings' hands curled around mine
    envision Peter walking through the front door
and utter words they have never
heard me say before.

"Not tonight."

Strings and Cans

During lunch
Matthew sits beside me
speaking words I would normally
find enticing.

Today
I look for my sister.

I'm surprised to find
she's looking back.

We gaze at each other
from opposite ends of the clearing
        exchange a sad smile
both feeling the empty space inside
where Peter should be.

I blink
against a flash of memory.

        Me and Dana as children
        making a phone
        out of strings and cans.

        Giggling,
        whispering secrets
        into the metal tins.

When Dana turns away,
I can still feel
the string between us.

Delicate,
breakable,
but there.

Angry

Tonight
something wakes me,
so bright and burning,
the insides of my eyelids
are shimmering and red.

I jerk upright,
see the inferno
the outside world has become.

Flames crackle
and blacken the window,
making glass hiss and fragment
like a spiderweb.

Terror expands in my throat,
blocking air and sound.

Then
I blink.

Everything
is the way it always was.

Dana snoring
    phone lines whispering
    clock ticking
    house creaking.

I notice something new
on the rug next to my bed.

My sock,
so small and forgotten,
charred and left for me to find.

An Embrace

In the morning
our father
walks through the door.

Abandoning their cereal,
Dana and Tyler
barrage him with questions.

After he satisfies them
with his answers,
my siblings leave
to tell friends the good news.

A relieved sigh
fills the room.

Then Dad shocks me
by walking to the table
        pulling me up
            wrapping his arms around me.

It's the first time
I've been hugged
in months.

He smells like medicine
and worry.

My father doesn't say a word
    doesn't voice his pain or doubt
but I feel it in his embrace.

I bury my fingers
into his sweater,
try not to think about the moment
he'll let me go.

A Choice

Word about Mary's party
spreads like butter over bread,
tempting and indulgent.

But I am distracted
by thoughts of the sock,
vanished off the rug
when I woke up
this morning.

After fourth period
Matthew walks next to me,
talks about numbers and goldfish.

The sound of his voice
slowly makes me forget
my troubles.

Then my brother spots us,
touches my elbow;
Matthew drifts ahead.

"Be careful, Fain," Tyler mutters.
"I don't want you to get hurt."

Beyond him,
hovering by her locker,
Mary Mosley scowls.

Then I see Matthew waiting for me
by the classroom doorway.

Our eyes meet
and I forget about all of it,
Tyler and Mary and warnings,
everything but the thrill
I feel right now.

The Teeth

My family is back together.

A week after
that terrible night,
everyone gathers around Peter
as if he is a flame
and this the coldest of nights.

We smile
    embrace
    kiss.

But the pneumonia
hasn't completely left his body
or our minds.

Suddenly this delicious moment
    so rare
    so new
is spoiled by a scream.

I jump,
leave my skin behind
as I run.

Dana stands in our room,
staring at the broken thing
that was once our window.

There's a warm presence
at my back,
and I turn.

"What happened?"
my father asks.

The jagged edges of the glass
rip and tear at me
like teeth.

I don't answer
        can't answer
and he hurries away
in search of something
to cover up the hole.

Dana follows him,
shouting for Tyler
to give her the phone.

For a few minutes
I stare into the darkness
that I usually find
so lovely.

It's no secret
who could have done this.

"You're jealous!" I shout
into the night;
breath leaves my mouth
in swirling clouds.

The monsters don't respond.

Sisters

It's the big night,
so big that it's a skyscraper
or a wish.

I stand in the bathroom
    curling iron in hand
    gritting my teeth
    glaring at the girl in the mirror
with her tangled, hopeless hair.

My sister appears in the doorway,
watches me for a moment.

Then, "Stop that. You're making it worse."

She takes the curling iron
    creases her brow
    concentrates.

Dana curls and teases my hair
until it is not hair anymore.

Finally she steps back,
waits for my reaction
with an expression that matches my own:
    wary
    uncertain
    hopeful.

"Thank you," I whisper,
words that I haven't uttered to my sister
in so long.

She shrugs
as if it's nothing,
but we both know
that's not true.

"Don't thank me yet," Dana mutters,
adjusting a curl at the back of my head.

When I ask her why,
she says, "We haven't touched your closet."

The Bus

Meet me there,
Matthew said.

But Mary Mosley's house
is across town.

Mom is too tired to drive,
Dad is snoring in their room,
Tyler is nowhere to be found,
Dana went off with her friends.

So I step outside
into the cool night air,
wait until the bus arrives.

The other passengers
sit weary and guarded
behind fences built of
books and screens and closed eyes.

I look around at
    a mother and her small son
    a white-haired man and his newspaper
    a man and his cell phone
    a boy and his bag of potato chips.

I imagine the world as a place
where you could sit down next to a stranger

and exist together
instead of separately.

For a moment or two,
I try to summon the nerve
to say hello.

After all,
I have swum through oceans
    walked the moon
    climbed up mountains.

In the end, though,
I listen to
    the murmurings of the mother
    the crinkling of the paper
    the chirps of the cell phone
    the crackling bag of chips
and stay silent in my seat.

Arrival

The house is like a castle,
all bricks and light and life.

I wear a mask of pretty makeup
    perfect hair
    seamless clothes.

After a moment,
I take a breath
    go up the stairs
    through the door.

The music
    is so loud
    that it pulses in my veins.

People gape
    stare
    whisper.

Their attention
makes me smile,
gives me courage.

I crane my neck,
try to find Matthew,
wonder if Anna will
be here, too.

I haven't seen her
since Halloween night.

There are so many people
    dancing and shouting and eating
it feels like we're trapped in a snow globe
that someone has shaken
hard and fast.

It's a good thing
I've always loved the snow.

The Blizzard

Lights flash,
the floor pounds,
my palms sweat,
courage fades.

I can't find
the boy from New Orleans,
see no sign of
the girl next door.

The snow
has become a blizzard,
howling and blinding.

Then
Mary's voice
sounds in my ear,
asks if I want some lemonade.

Before I can answer,
she pushes a red plastic cup
into my hand.

Her eyes are wide
and bright
as she drinks,
so I do, too.

It's fruity,
like the hard candies
Peter got on Halloween.

I notice some girls whispering,
pointing to an unlocked cabinet
at the far end of the room.

Then somehow the cup is empty
and another is pushed at me.

I gulp and gulp and gulp,
swallowing my nerves
with each one.

My classmates are laughing,
and everything is so funny and fuzzy,
it's hard to remember
what I was worried about in the first place.

I am tingling,
I want to dance.

Suddenly
I love the world so much,
and I hate it, too.

Why is it so hard
to figure out where
and how to belong?

But here and now
among my peers,
    I am strong
    I am visible
    I am welcome.

Then
I am puking.

A Closed Door

It's not over.

All my feelings
rush up inside me,
a thick, burning river.

A hand holds my hair
and I see there's a mess on the carpet.

"Bathroom," I manage.

"She's going to hurl again!" someone shrieks.

They step back
as if I'm a bomb
about to explode.

Someone helps me
up the stairs.

I throw open the first door I find,
stumble into the darkness,
turn on the light.

Instead of a toilet
I see the boy from New Orleans
pressed up against the wall
        and the lips of Mary Mosley.

She steps back,
annoyed at the interruption,
their mouths pink
from stolen kisses.

Matthew stares at me,
his hair ruffled and adorable.

Suddenly I need to throw up
for a completely different reason.

I turn and run.

"Fain, wait!" he says.

There's an angry exclamation from Mary,
the sound of Matthew's pursuit.

I rush past Anna,
realize she's the one
who held my hair
and helped me up the stairs.

I move too fast
to stop or speak.

Even without a destination
or escape plan,
only one thought,
steady as a drum,

beats through me:
away.

I wonder how anyone
ever thought the
world was flat;
I feel it spin beneath me
as I totter off balance.

Stumble into the kitchen,
reach for the doorknob
that leads to the backyard.

A hand catches hold of my arm,
stops me.

"Fain, wait!" Matthew says again.

I slowly turn to face him,
a joke with my puke-covered shirt
and throbbing heart.

"Sorry you had to see that . . . Mary gets intense sometimes . . ."

Clumsily
he weaves together
an explanation.

"Intense?"

I am a parrot or a canyon,
only capable of echoes.

Something in my face
must make Matthew realize.
"You thought . . ."

His words stop short,
too hard for him to say,
harder still for me to hear.

He swallows,
eyes dimming
before they dart away.

"We're friends, Fain," he says.

But no.
He is not my friend.
My friends arrive with the stars.

I walk away,
and for the first time
I don't turn around
when he calls my name.

Arms

I wake on the grass,
my skin made of ice,
everything else numb.

I have a vague memory
of holding a phone in my hand.

Now something is happening all around,
voices and shadows arguing.

Tyler is here,
his words sharper
than all the knives in Mom's cupboard.

Arms wrap around me
    help me
    guide me.

I tell the blurry faces
how much I wish I had their arms
before all this.

They put me in the car,
whisper soothingly,
bring me home.

They tuck me into bed,
put a bowl by my head,
say they'll see me in the morning,
retreat until only one shadow is left.

A distant part of me
recognizes my sister,
as though I'm standing on an opposite shore
peering through the fog.

"What happened?" she whispers,
draping a blanket over me.

"Nothing."

"You can tell me the truth," she says.

But the truth
has been trapped inside me
so long
that to let it out
would be like vomiting again.

So instead I say,
"I hate how loud you snore."

Dana blinks in surprise,
and before she can respond
I turn over,
succumb to the dark.

The Morning After

The sun is my enemy.

I focus on the pain
in my head
so that nothing else
can make its way in.

No memories of yesterday,
no thoughts of today,
no worries of tomorrow.

I sense that I am not alone,
roll onto my side.

Dana gazes at me
from across the room,
without a trace of
disappointment or judgment
in her eyes.

She looks at me differently,
as if she's really seeing me
for the first time.

After a minute she says, "I'll get some nasal strips."

It's so unexpected,
it takes me a while to respond.

"That would be good," I finally say.

Without another word,
Dana gets up
and shuts the curtains
to block out the morning light.

The Hole

There is a hole
in my chest
where my heart
has been ripped out.

I don't know why
people call it heartbreak
when there's nothing left
to crack.

Brother

I stay in bed all day,
replaying the scene with
Matthew and Mary
over and over
in my mind.

At dusk
     a time of yellowness
     and tears
someone fills the doorway.

My heart becomes a star,
soaring bright with hope.

Maybe Matthew has realized
his true feelings
for me.

When I see it's only Tyler,
my heart falls,
crashes to the Earth
in a blend of dirt and fire.

He shoves his hands
in his pockets
     looks at his feet
     clears his throat.

I hug my pillow,
wait for his *I told you so,*
but my older brother has never
been a boy of many words.

Instead
Tyler sits on the bed,
stays with me
even when the sun is gone.

Promises

Voices drift down the hallway;
I hear my name.

My mind is consumed
by ugly truths,
painful memories of
     sickly sweet drinks
     swollen lips
     averting gazes.

Ignoring my family,
I lie in bed,
face turned
to the window.

I hear her enter softly,
close my eyes,
pretend to sleep.

Dana kneels,
touches my hand.

When I don't answer,
she makes another promise.

This time she vows
to be a better sister.

I almost open my eyes,
tell her I never wanted
a better sister.

I just wanted her.

Unknown

Monday morning,
a familiar head of hair appears
at the far end of the hall.

I wave,
want to thank her for helping
me at Mary's party,
but she avoids my gaze,
rushes past.

There's something
in the hunch of her shoulders,
the lines around her mouth
that I have never seen before.

I think about it in class
    at the quarry
    on the walk home.

It isn't until the sun sinks
that I comprehend
the look on her face,
but it's one I don't understand.

Guilt.

Messages

When I get home from school,
the carpet
is covered in snowflakes.

There is something familiar about them,
but I don't realize what it is
until I see my brother on the couch,
scissors in his hand.

He has
folded and sliced
my stories
into winter.

"No, Peter!" I cry,
yank the scissors
from his grasp.

He yells at me
and I yell back.

Mom soon appears,
demanding silence
so she can sleep
before her shift.

I scoop up scraps of paper,
flee.

Snowflakes trail behind me,
flutter to the floor,
realer than the threat of winter,
and I feel my lip tremble.

The words
are cut up beyond repair,
no hope
of putting them back.

I place my hand
against the frost-covered window,
ask the monsters
to come back to me.

Then I crawl
into bed.

Return

Claws scrape
against my windowsill.

Then, a voice,
raspy, childlike, familiar.

By the time I reach the window,
grateful tears
stream down my face,
make everything hazy.

They know
about Matthew.

"We'll eat his flesh!"
"Suck the marrow from his bones!"
"Carve out his eyes!"

Smiling,
I just shake my head.

Then,
as if no time at all has passed,
we go outside,
have grand adventures
on the stars.

Their laughter is loud,
wind and magic endless,
the moon beautifully bright.

I try to enjoy
our night in the sky,
but I can't stop myself
from thinking about
what and who
I've left behind.

Gestures

The moon watches
as I return to my bed,
curling beneath the blankets,
hugging my pillow.

There's a crumpling sound,
a gentle touch
against my cheek.

When I open my eyes
I see Peter holding
snowflakes,
taped together
into the shape of my stories.

It's a truce
an apology
a gift.

I hug him so tightly
it must hurt,
but my brother
doesn't complain.

Up

In the morning
I open my eyes,
and this time
I keep them open.

The world out there
is so vast and unknown,
but also smaller
than I ever imagined.

There is still a hole in my chest
    still a need to squint in the light
    still an instinct to bury myself under the covers.

But I swing my legs
to the side,
stand anyway.

Warrior

It is the last week of school
before Thanksgiving break.

I sit in class,
studiously avoiding
the stares and whispers
that haven't stopped
since the night of the party.

I can't bring myself
to look at Matthew or Mary;
Anna's still avoiding me.

Halfway through the hour
someone puts a drawing
down in front of me.

I look at Carl,
who looks back
with honest eyes.

I turn my gaze
to the lines of his pen,
see what he's created.

He's drawn a picture of me,
a version of myself
I have never known:

his Fain is not lonely
or timid.

She is a warrior
with a flashing sword,
streaming hair,
expression fierce.

I know
she can do anything.

I lift my head
to thank Carl
but he is already drawing again,
putting his own truths to paper
where anyone
who cares to look
can see them.

Twisted Sheets

I am standing
on a mountain made of tongues,
all of them wriggling,
shouting at me
in a thousand different languages.

I am walking
down a street
empty of all but
    wistful breezes
    sighing stars
    creaking doors.

I am being eaten
alive by crows,
their beaks
pecking and poking and tearing.

I am in a grave
with the bell rope
next to my hand,
but I can't move
to ring it.

And then I am being shaken awake,
listening to a low whisper
that tells me everything is all right,
I'm safe.

"Mom?" I whisper,
open my eyes
to her dim outline.

"You were having a bad dream," she says,
her palm a cool spot
on my skin.

I grab her hand
and hold it tight,
reassure myself
this isn't another dream.

"Don't leave," I say.

She doesn't speak,
just slides down
into the space beside me,
tucks the covers
around us both.

She reeks
of cheeseburgers and coffee,
but I don't mind one bit.

For a few minutes
we breathe in sync,
    Dana still sound asleep
till I feel myself
slipping away.

Then a movement
yanks me back
to the present;
my mother twitches and smiles
as if she's caught
in a thrilling dream.

I wonder
if she's floated amongst
the stars, too.

Fruit

At breakfast
I find an apple
in the fridge.

Think of the boy
from New Orleans,
hesitate,
put it back.

Take
an orange instead.

Wings

Today
the cafeteria is
made of only eyes and whispers.

My tree
seems far away
now that the teachers
have deemed it too cold
to eat outside.

Matthew sits in the corner
with Mary Mosley,
a king on his plastic throne.

I hesitate,
clutch my tray.

He catches my stare.

Even now
the sight of him
makes the birds in my stomach
flutter.

Anna sits beside them,
looks at me,
struggle written plainly
across her face.

We both know
she doesn't belong
with the Mary Mosleys
of the world.

But sometimes it feels impossible
to leave the familiar behind.

I can't help her;
there are some battles
we must fight on our own.

Then,
a voice.

"Fain! Sit with me," Dana demands.

I settle under
my sister's wing,
tucked around me
warm and safe.

The Rink

That night
I open my eyes to once again see
my sister's face above me,
a pale moon rising
over the horizon
of our room.

"Get up," Dana orders.

She won't answer any questions,
but I ask them all the same.

By the time I get to the door,
she and Tyler
are already there.

The three of us
sneak out,
walk the six blocks
to the rink.

Our snow pants swish,
heavy boots clomp.

We creep onto the ice
and our bladeless feet
don't matter:

we fall
and laugh
and glide
and spin.

Every time
I hit the ground,
they reach down
and pull me up.

All my nights
with the monsters
cannot compare to this.

Endings

Later that night
the monsters visit me
even though I haven't called them.

Still,
I take hold of their hands
and climb back out
into the cold.

The dongs of the clock
fade fast behind us.

The monsters
are more fearless than usual.

We fly with a flock of honking geese
across the midnight moon.

     I think of gliding over ice,
     holding tight to Dana and Tyler.

We have a tea party
in the middle of a cloud.

     I think of building towers and trick-or-treating
     with Peter.

We run into the forest
and hunt with wolves.

     I think of tucking my head into the warm curve
     of my mother's neck.

We tie a balloon around an elephant's belly,
watch it ascend into the stars.

     I think of the constellations,
     talking with Anna in the dark.

Our journeys are just as magical
as they have ever been,
but nothing feels the same.

All the while
we fly and chase and run,
my favorite monster is silent.

When I ask him
what has changed,
he gives me a sad smile.

"You."

In that moment I know
that my little monsters
will never tap on the window again.

Reconciliations

I look out the window
toward the street,
and there she is.

We meet
in the spot
where we first met.

Where I saw
her swollen eyes
and she just saw
me for me.

Her scarf flutters
in the breeze.

"It was my fault," Anna blurts,
her cheeks flushed with shame.
"I told Mary which window was yours."

Then she apologizes,
asks if she can eat lunch with me
tomorrow.

I consider this
for a moment.

"I want to show you something," I say.

Ripples

When we arrive,
Anna looks around with so much curiosity,
it's as though she's examining
my soul.

She picks up a rock,
throws it with all the strength
in her arm.

"What is this place?" she asks.

"Quiet," I answer,
tracking the progress
of a seagull as it
flies across the sky.

I tell her
I used to come here
when I needed
someplace safe.

We stand silently,
look out over the water
for a while.

"If a bird stops flying,
does that mean
it's no longer a bird?" Anna asks.

I'm not sure
if she expects an answer,
but a ripple
expands over the water
in response.

This doesn't feel
like my haven anymore;
now it just feels empty.

Minutes pass;
Anna and I leave the quarry,
a place of escape and loneliness.

I will not be back.

Rebuilding

The sound of my brother's giggle
draws me to his bedroom door.

Unaware of my presence,
Peter looks out the window,
smiling and touching that fragile barrier.

The city we once so painstakingly built
crumbled and forgotten
on the floor.

I ask my brother
what it is
that made him laugh.

"Squirrel," he says, grinning.

I follow his gaze
but see only quivering branches,
roiling skies.

"Come with me," I say,
taking his small hand.

When Peter is not looking,
I unlock the window.

Just in case.

Second Chances

A space heater hums
as I walk down the stairs,
step closer,
magazine crinkling
in my hands.

"Are you awake?" I whisper.
"Can I show you something?"

My mother stirs
from her place on the couch,
lifts her head,
squints at me.

"What is it?" she mumbles.

Ignoring the instinct
to turn and run,
I put my story on her lap.

Mom is so silent, so still,
the light inside me
begins to fade.

But then she rubs her eye with one knuckle
and sits up
for a better look.

I know the exact moment
she sees my name
and realizes what it is
she's holding.

"Honey!" she shouts.
"Come look at this!"

Dad

There are some stories
without happy endings.

There are some tales
that go on and on.

It happens gradually,
like the seasons changing
    bones growing.

Every day I go into the kitchen
and I see the tiny differences
in my family
    far from perfect
    but still trying
growing taller and stronger
like Peter's tower of blocks.

Tyler kneels down
to pick up
the spoon our brother dropped.

Dana ignores
the ringing phone,
talks about the upcoming dance.

At the stove,
Mom takes a moment

to turn her head
and smile at me.

But all the while
Dad sits at the table
rubbing his head,
staring at the tiny letters
of the classifieds.

I don't know
if he'll stay in that chair
or if one day I'll come home
to find it empty.

For now
all that matters is
it isn't.

Thanksgiving

Steam rises off the turkey,
condensation rolls down the water pitcher,
forks clink against plates.

My prize-winning story
hangs on the wall
in a brand-new frame.

It's the first meal
our family has had together
since I can remember.

I hope it's not the last.

In the middle of dessert,
the room goes bright
and I realize
it's snowing again.

Normally
I would lose myself
in the magic
outside the window.

But the scene around me
is so beautiful,
I find that
I cannot look away.

Dancing

Dana has been making plans.

She planned our dresses
　　our ride
　　our night.

But I've made plans
of my own.

We're in the gymnasium,
where I once felt so apart
from everything.

Stars dangle from the ceiling,
a band plays,
lights swoop and flash.

It takes me a while
to find the boy
who saw the Fain no one else did.

"Will you dance with me?" I ask Carl.

Smooth my skirt,
wonder if he will notice
that it's as silver
as the armor he drew me in.

Eyes watch from all around
as we dance
with pride
    joy
        abandon.

Then Anna finds me,
loops her arm
through mine,
white teeth gleaming in laughter.

Dana elbows through,
and moments later
Tyler pushes his way
into our circle.

Suddenly I realize
I no longer feel alone.

Apologies

Fingers brush my arm,
cold and clammy.

Somehow I know
before I turn around
it's the boy
from New Orleans.

"Hi, Fain."

He fidgets;
his suit doesn't fit right,
just like us.

Mary Mosley
stands a short distance away,
sour-faced;
I wonder if anyone
has made her drink
lemonade tonight.

"Listen," Matthew starts.

His words are strange
with their hidden meanings
and murky intentions.

I glance over my shoulder,
see my friends, my siblings
waiting.

"Tell it to the goldfish," I say.

A Gift

During a still moment
something draws me
to the woods.

I find the clearing
where I once danced
around a fire
with monsters.

I kneel to the ground
and pick up a stick,
recognize it as
my former queenly scepter.

A few yards away
rests an upturned bucket,
plastic and cracked.

I know it will fit as effortlessly
as the crown I once wore.

I make a pile of it all
in case someone else needs it
someday.

Then I sit against a tree,
write a different kind
of story.

I write about
    a girl who is learning
            to take things as they come
    a girl who is learning
            that life is far from perfect.

But she's also learning
that things are constantly
    changing
    shifting
    growing
every moment of every day.

Then I close my notebook,
leave the woods,
run all the way home.

Acknowledgments

It may seem strange that I worked harder on this book than any other, because there are significantly fewer words involved. But each of those words were examined and agonized over to make *The Lonely Ones* the best it could possibly be, and that wouldn't have happened without certain people. My thanks and eternal appreciation go to:

Liza Kaplan, not only for her passion during this process but also for being so understanding when I needed extra time to work on Fain's story. She is an incredible editor to work with, and I'm constantly pinching myself to make sure all of this is real. The bruises reassure me that, yes, she really is in my corner and this whole thing happened.

My amazing agent, Beth Miller, for not batting an eyelash when I sent her this manuscript out of the blue. The day before she was leaving on holiday, no less. "I don't know what this is, really, but what do you think?" I wrote. That very same day she replied with, "Okay, so I love this a lot." Neither of us had explored novels in verse before, but Beth didn't let that stop her for a second. She really does have superpowers.

Talia Benamy and Michael Green, for their time and dedication.

Kristy King, for her excellent feedback on the very, very rough first draft. So much of what she said helped shape what this book has become.

Jordan Kralewski and Emily Neuman, who both spent many long afternoons with me as I worked on this book. Thank you for letting me bounce ideas off you, for closing my Facebook and Pinterest windows when the time called for it, and ultimately keeping me sane during revisions. And Jordan, thank you for the hot chocolate. It was an essential part of the process.

Larry Swain, for his patience and encouragement during my internship with him. I may have missed a couple deadlines while struggling to meet the one for this manuscript. I'll be eternally grateful for the day when he said, "Okay, Sutton, forget the essay. Your focus for the next couple weeks will be getting this book done."

Theresa Evangelista and Siobhán Gallagher, for designing such a lovely book to go along with the story.

I wouldn't have been able to do this without any of you.

DATE DUE